Grandmother's Tale

Indian Thought Publications

Other works by Narayan in this imprint

Novels

Swami and Friends
The Bachelor of Arts
The Dark Room
The English Teacher
Mr. Sampath - The Printer of Malgudi
The Financial Expert
Waiting for the Mahatma
The Man-eater of Malgudi
The Guide
The Painter of Signs
A Tiger for Malgudi
Talkative Man
The World of Nagaraj
The Vendor of Sweets

Short Stories

Malgudi Days
Under the Banyan Tree and Other Stories

Autobiography

My Days

Grandmother's Tale

R.K.Narayan

Sketches by

R.K.Laxman

Indian Thought Publications

INDIAN THOUGHT PUBLICATIONS
Registered office : 38, Thanikachalam Road, T Nagar, Madras - 600 017
Administrative office : Surya Castle, F2, 1st Floor, Old No: 26/New No: 30, West Road, West CIT Nagar, Madras - 600 035
Phone : 044 -28344512 Email: service@kkbooks.com
Web: www.kkbooks.com

Grandmother's Tale

ISBN: 978-81-85986-15-9

First Indian Edition 1992
31st Reprint, 2024

Printed in India at
Sudarsan Graphics Private Limited
4/641, 12th Link Street, Kottivakkam (OMR), Chennai - 600 041
www.sudarsan.com

To

K Krishnamurthy

who persuaded me

to write this book

EXPLANATION

The borderline between fact and fiction, between biography and tale wears thin and ultimately vanishes in the following chronicle. Readers are bound to question how much of it is history and how much is fiction. I do not know the answer myself. The composition grew as I wrote it from my grandmother's narration, in daily instalments, of her mother's search for her errant husband, who left no address after uttering a laconic good-bye, "I am going away." That it might not all be imaginary could be concluded from the fact that the descendants of the couple in the story are present in our midst in different walks of life, scattered here and there, with this author being one of them.

Grandmother's Tale

I was brought up by my grandmother in Madras from my third year while my mother lived in Bangalore with a fourth child on hand after me. My grandmother took me away to Madras in order to give relief to an over-burdened daughter.

My grandmother Ammani was a busy person. She performed a variety of tasks all through the day, cooking and running the house for her two sons, gardening, counselling neighbours and the tenants living in the rear portion of the vast house stretching away in several segments, settling disputes, studying horoscopes and arranging matrimonial alliances. At the end of the day she settled down on a swing – a broad plank suspended by chains from the ceiling; lightly propelling it with her feet back and forth, chewing betel, she was completely relaxed at that hour. She held me at her side and taught me songs, prayers, numbers, and the alphabet till supper-time.

I mention 'supper-time', but there was no fixed supper-time. My uncles returned home late in the evening. The senior uncle conducted a night school for slum children. (Some of them, later in life, attained eminence as *pundits* in Tamil language and literature.) The junior uncle worked in the harbour as a stevedore's assistant and came home at uncertain hours. Supper-time could be based not on their home-coming but on my performance. My grandmother fed me only when I completed my lessons to her satisfaction.

I had to repeat the multiplication table up to twenty but I always fumbled and stuttered after twelve and needed prodding and goading to attain the peak; I had to recite Sanskrit verse and *slokas* in praise of Goddess Saraswathi and a couple of other gods, and hymns in Tamil; identify six *ragas* when granny hummed the tunes or, conversely, mention the songs when she named the *ragas*; and then solve arithmetic problems such as, "If a boy wants four mangoes costing one *anna* per mango, how much money will he have to take?" I wanted to blurt out, "Boys don't have to buy, they can obtain a fruit with a well-aimed stone at a mango tree." I brooded and blinked without a word, afraid I might offend her if I mentioned the stone technique for obtaining a fruit. She watched me and then tapping my skull gently remarked, "Never seen a bigger dunce ..."

It was all very taxing, I felt hungry and sleepy. To keep me awake, she kept handy a bowl of cold water and sprinkled it on my eye-lids from time to time.

I could not understand why she bothered so much to make me learned. She also taught me some folk songs which now, I realize, were irrelevant, such as the one about a drunkard sleeping indifferently while his child in the crib was crying and the mother was boiling the milk. The most unnecessary lesson however, in my memory as I realize it now, was a Sanskrit lyric, not in praise of God, but defining the perfect woman – it said the perfect woman must work like a slave, advise like a *Mantri* (Minister), look like Goddess Lakshmi, be patient like Mother Earth and courtesan-like in the bed chamber – this I had to recite on certain days of the week. After the lessons she released me and served food. When I was six years old I was ceremoniously escorted to the Lutheran Mission School nearby and admitted in the "Infant Standard."

Later I grew up in Mysore, with my parents visiting my grandmother in Madras once a year during the holidays. After completing my college course, I frequently visited Madras to try my luck as a free-lance writer.

My junior uncle, no longer a stevedore's

assistant but an automobile salesman for a German make, set out every morning to contact his 'prospects' and demonstrate the special virtues of his car. He took me out with him, saying "If you want to be a writer, don't mope at home listening to grandmother's tales. You must be up and doing; your B.A. degree will lead you nowhere if you do not contact 'prospects'. Come out with me and watch ..." He drove me about, stopped here and there, met all sorts of persons and delivered his sales talk, making sure that I followed his performance intelligently. I avoided his company in the evenings, since he wined and dined with his 'prospects' to clinch a sale. During his morning rounds, however, I went out with him to be introduced to men who, he thought, were in the writing line. He left me in their company to discuss my literary aspirations. Most of them were printers, established in the highways and byways of the city, or publishers of almanacs, diaries, lottery tickets and race-cards, who were looking for proof-readers on a daily wage of ten rupees.

My uncle urged me to accept any offer that came: "You must make a start and go up. Do you know what I was earning when I worked at the harbour? Less than twenty five a month, in addition to occasional tips from clearing agents. That is how I learnt my job. Then I moved on to a job at a bookshop on Mount Road, cycling up in the morning, with a lunch packet in hand, and selling books till seven in the evening. It was hard work, but I was learning a job. Today, do you know what I get? One thousand for every car I sell, in addition to expenses for entertaining the prospects. You will have to learn your job while earning whatever the wages might be. That is how you should proceed."

After brooding over these suggestions, I began to ignore his advice and stayed at home much to his annoyance: "Well, if you do not want to prosper, I will just say G.T.H. (go to hell), I have better things to do ..." (However, he relented subsequently after the publication of my novels, the first three, in England.) In 1940, when I started a quarterly journal *Indian Thought* in Mysore, he took it upon himself to help its circulation, applying his sales talk at high pressure. Carrying a sample copy of *Indian Thought* from door to door, he booked one thousand subscribers in Madras city alone in the first year. Unfortunately, *Indian Thought* ceased publication in the second year since I could not continue it single-handed.

Although ageing, my grandmother was still active and concerned herself with other people's affairs, her domestic drudgery now mitigated by the presence of two daughters-in-law in the house. She sat as usual on the swing in the evenings, invited me to sit beside her, and narrated stories of her early days – rather of her mother's early life and adventures, as heard from her mother when Ammani was about ten years old.

Day after day, I sat up with her listening to the account, and at night developed it as a cogent narrative. As far as possible, I have tried to retain the flavour of her speech, though the manner of her narrative could not be reproduced as it proceeded in several directions back and forth and got mixed up with asides and irrelevancies. I have managed to keep her own words here and there, but this is mainly a story-writer's version of a hearsay biography of a great-grandmother.

She was seven when she was married, her husband being just ten years old. Those were days of child marriages, generally speaking. Only widowers re-married late in life. It is not possible for me to fix the historical background by any clue or internal evidence. My grandmother could not be specific about the time since she was unborn at the beginning of her mother's story. One has to assume an arbitrary period – that is the later period of the East India Company, before the Sepoy Mutiny.

My grandmother could not specify the location

of their beginnings. It might be anywhere in the Southern Peninsula. She just mentioned it as "that village", which conjures up a familiar pattern: a hundred houses scattered in four or five narrow streets, with pillared *verandas* and *pyols,* massive front doors, inner courtyards, situated at the bend of a river or its tributary, mounds of garbage here and there, cattle everywhere, a temple tower looming over it all, the temple hall and corridor serving as a meeting ground for the entire population, and an annual festival attracting a big crowd from nearby hamlets – an occasion when a golden replica of the deity in the inner shrine was carried in a procession with pipes and drums around the village. "What God was He ?" I could not resist my curiosity; my grandmother knew as much as I did, but ventured a guess, "Could be Ranganatha, the aspect of Vishnu in repose in a state of *yoga* lying on the coils of the thousand-headed Adisesha. The God was in a trance and watched and protected our village. They were married in the temple – my father and mother. Don't interrupt me with questions, as I have also only heard about these events. My mother told me that she was playing in the street with her friends one evening when her father came up and said, 'You are going to be married today next week'."

"Why ?" she asked and did not get an answer.

Her father ignored her questions and went away. Her playmates stopped their game, surrounded and teased her, "Hey bride! Hey bride!"

"Wait! You will also be brides soon!" she retorted and rushed back home to her mother, crying, "Whatever happens, I am not going to marry. My friends are making fun of me!" Her mother soothed her and explained patiently that she was old enough to marry, something that could not be avoided by any human being, an occasion when she would be showered with gifts and new clothes and gold ornaments. The girl, however, was not impressed. She sulked and wept in a corner of their home. After fixing the date of the wedding, they kept her strictly indoors and did not allow her to go out and play. Her playmates visited her and whispered their sympathies.

On an auspicious day she was clad in a saree, decked in jewellery and taken to the pillared hall of the temple where had gathered guests and relations and priests, a piper and drummer creating enough noise to drown the uproar of the priests chanting *mantras* and the babble of the guests. She was garlanded and made to sit beside a boy whom she had often noticed tossing a rubber ball in an adjoining street whenever she went out to buy a pencil, ribbon or sweets in a little shop. She felt shy to look at him now, sitting

too close to him on a plank. The smoke from the holy fire smarted her eyes and also created a smoke-screen blurring her vision whenever she stole a glance in his direction.

At the auspicious hour the piper, drummer and the chanting priests combined to create the maximum din as Viswa approached the girl, seated on her father's lap, and tied the yellow thread around her neck – and they became man and wife from that moment.

In a week all celebration, feasting and exchange of ceremonial visits between the bride and bridegroom parties ceased. Viswanath the bridegroom went back to his school run by a pedagogue on a brick platform under a banyan tree on the riverside. He was ragged by his class-fellows for getting married. He denied it and became violent till the pedagogue intervened and brought his cane down the back of a teasing member. The boy said between sobs, "He is lying. I was at the temple with my father and ate, along with the others, a big feast with four kinds of sweets. Viswanath wore new clothes, a gold chain and a big garland around his neck. If I am lying, let him take off his shirt and show us the sacred thread ..." He bared his chest and held up his sacred thread to demonstrate that he had only a bachelor's three-strand thread.

The teacher was old, suffered from sore-throat, and could not control his class of twenty five children when a babble broke out on the subject of Viswa's marriage. A few cried, "Shame, shame," which was the usual form of greeting in their society. The teacher tapped his cane on the floor and cried out over the tumult, "Why shame? I was married when I was like Viswa. I have four sons and two daughters and grandchildren. My wife looks after those at home still, and runs the family; and they will all marry soon. There is no shame in marriage. It's all arranged by the God in that temple. Who are we to say anything against His will? My wife was also small when we married ..."

The girl's life changed after her marriage. She could not go out freely, or join her friends playing in the street. She could not meet her husband, except on special occasions such as the New Year and other festival days when Viswa was invited to visit his wife's home with his parents. On those occasions, the girl was kept aloof in a separate room and would be escorted to his presence by young women who would giggle and urge the young couple to say something to each other and then leave them alone for a little time.

The couple felt embarrassed and shy and tongue-tied but took that opportunity to study each other's features. When they got a chance, the very first sentence the girl uttered was, "There is a black patch under your ear." She made bold to touch his face with her forefinger. Apart from holding each other's right hand before the holy fire during their wedding ceremony, this was their first touch. He found that her finger was soft and she found the skin under his left ear rough but pleasant. When she removed her finger she asked, "What is this patch?" She thrust her finger again to trace that black patch under his left ear. "Oh, that!" he said pressing down her finger on the black patch. "It's a lucky sign, my mother says."

"Does it hurt?" she asked solicitously.

"No. They say it's lucky to have that mark," he said.

"How much luck?" she asked and continued, "Will you become a king?"

"Yes, that's what they say." And before they could develop this subject, others opened the door and came in, not wanting to leave the couple alone too long.

After that they discovered an interest in each other's company. But it was not easy to meet. It was impossible for the girl to go out, unless chaperoned by an elder of the family. Even such outings were limited to a visit to the temple on a

Friday evening or to a relation on ceremonial occasions. Viswa wished he could be told when and where he could see her. Occasionally he found an excuse to visit her home on the pretext of wanting to meet his father-in-law but it did not always work as that man would be away in his coconut grove far away.

Viswa did not possess the hardihood to step into the house to catch a glimpse of his young wife. She kept herself in the deepest recess of the house for fear of being considered too forward and he would turn back disappointed. But he soon found a way. He spied and discovered that she was more accessible at their backyard, where she washed clothes at the well. There was only a short wall separating their backyard from a lane, which proved a more convenient approach since he could avoid a neighbour always lounging on the *pyol* and asking, "Ay ! Visiting your wife ! Insist upon a good tiffin ..." It made him self-conscious. He would simper and murmur and hasten his steps only to be met by his mother-in-law at the door. Now the backyard could be approached without anyone accosting him, but the lane was dirty and garbage-ridden; he did not mind it. On his way back from school if he took a diversion, he could approach the lane and the short wall. He placed a couple of bricks close to the wall, stood on the pile with his head showing

up a few inches above it. It was a sound strategy though her back was turned to him, while she drew water from the well and filled a bucket and soaked her clothes. He watched her for a few moments and cried, "Hey!" When she did not hear his call, he clapped his hands, and she turned and stared at him. He said, "Hey! I am here."

Looking back watchfully into their house she asked, "Why?"

"To see you," he said.

"Come by the front door," she said.

And he said promptly, "I can't. It's no good. How arc you? I came to ask," he said rather timidly.

"Why should you ask?" she questioned. He had no immediate answer. He just blinked. She laughed at him and said, "You are tall today."

"Yes," he said, "Is your name Balambal? It's too long."

"Call me Bala," she said, picked up her bucket and suddenly retreated into the house. He waited, hoping she would come back. But the back door shut with a bang, and he jumped off muttering, "She is funny. I should not have married her. But what could I do? I was never asked whether I wanted to marry or not ..." He ran down the lane and sought the company of his friend Ramu, who lived in a house next to the temple and knew when the *pujas* at the temple were performed and when they would distribute the offerings, sweet rice and coconut pieces. If one stuck to Ramu, one need not starve for snacks. He could take Viswa to see the God at the appropriate moment when the evening service was in progress and wait. After the waving of camphor flames and the sounding of cymbals and bells, the offerings would be distributed. Piously standing on the threshold of the sanctum, Ramu would whisper, "Viswa, shut your eyes and pray, otherwise they will not give you anything to eat!"

At the next session he was more successful. Standing on the pile of bricks, he told her: "On Tuesday evening I went to the temple."

"Did you pray? What for?" she asked. Seeing his silence, she said, "Why go to temple if you don't pray?"

"I don't know any prayer."

"What did you learn at home?"

He realized she was a heckler and tried to ward off the attack. "I know some prayers, not all."

"Recite some," she said.

"No, I won't," he said resolutely.

"You will be sent to hell if you don't say your prayers."

"How do you know?" he asked.

"My mother has told me. She makes us all pray in the evenings in the *puja* room."

"Bah!" he said. "What do you get to eat after the prayers? At the temple if you shut your eyes and prostrate before the God, they give you wonderful things to eat. For that you must come with me and Ramu ..."

"Who is Ramu?"

"My friend." Viswa said and jumped off the pile of bricks as there were portents of the girl's mother appearing on the scene. He was now satisfied that he had been able to establish a line of communication with Bala although the surroundings were filthy and he had to tread warily lest he should put his foot on excreta, since the lane served as the public convenience.

They could not meet normally as husband and wife. Bala, being only ten years old, must attain puberty and then go through an elaborate nuptial ceremony before she could join her husband.

Viswa had other plans. One afternoon he stood on the brick-pile and beckoned her. She looked up and frantically signalled to him to go away. "I have to talk to you," he said desperately and ducked and crouched while her mother appeared at the door for a moment. After she had gone in, he heard a soft voice calling, "Hey, speak."

His head bobbed up again over the wall and he just said: "I am going away. Keep it a secret ..."

"Where are you going?"

"I don't know. Far away."

"Why?"

He had no answer. He merely said, "Even Ramu doesn't know."

"Who are you going with?"

"I don't know but I am joining some pilgrims beyond the river."

"Won't you tell me why you are going away?"

"No. I can't ... I have to go away – that is all."

"Can't you mention a place where you are going?"

"I don't know ..."

She began to laugh. "Oh! Oh! you are going to 'I don't know' place. Is that it?"

He felt irked by her levity and said, "I don't know really. They were a group of pilgrims singing a *bhajan* about Pandaripura or some such place ... over and over again."

"Are you sure?"

"You won't see me for a long time ..."

"But when will you come back?"

"Later," he said and vanished as he noticed her mother coming again and that was the last the girl saw of him for a long time to come.

She remained indifferent for a week or ten days and then began secretly to worry. She thought at first Viswa was playing a joke and would re-appear over the wall sooner or later. She wanted to tell her mother, but was afraid she might begin to investigate how she came to know Viswa had disappeared, and then proceed to raise the wall to keep him off. She suffered silently, toyed with the idea of seeking Ramu's help but she had never seen him. Others at home did not bother. Her father was, as ever, interested only in his coconut grove, the price of coconut, coconut pests and so on. He left home at dawn after breakfasting on rice soaked overnight in cold water, packed a lunch and returned home at night tired, leaving domestic matters to his wife's care.

Bala's mother noticed her brooding silence and gloom and asked one day, "What is ailing you?"

Bala burst into tears "He ... He ... is gone," she said.

"Who?"

Bala replied, "He ... He ..." since a wife could not utter her husband's name. When Bala's father returned home from the garden, the lady told him "Viswa has disappeared." He took it lightly and said, "Must be playing with his friends somewhere, where could he go? How do you know he has disappeared?"

"I have not seen him for a long time. He used to come up to see you, but as you were always away, he would turn back from the door."

"Poor boy! You should have called him in... Young people are shy!"

"Bala also shut herself in whenever he came ..."

"She is also young and shy ... I must take him with me to the grove some time." The lady persuaded the man to stay away from the coconut grove the next morning and they went over to Viswa's house. "After all they are our *sambandis* (relations through a matrimonial alliance) and we must pay them courtesy visits at least once in a while."

Viswa's parents lived in what was named Chariot Nook (where the temple chariot was stationed in a shed).

After a formal welcome and the courtesy of unrolling a mat for the visitors, Viswa's father and Bala's father asked simultaneously, "Where is Viswa?" When they realized no one knew the answer, Viswa's parents said, "We thought he was in your house. We were planning to come and see him."

Next they visited the school-master, who said he had not seen Viswa for more than ten days.

It became a sensation in the village. Well-wishers of the family and others crowded in,

speculating, sympathising, and suggesting the next step, vociferous and excited and talking simultaneously. A little fellow in the crowd said, "I saw him with a group crossing the river ..."

"When?"

"I don't remember."

"Didn't you talk to him?"

"Yes, he said he was going to Delhi." There was ironic laughter at this. "Delhi is thousands of miles away ..."

"More."

"I hear sepoys are killing white officers."

"Who told you?"

"Someone from the town ..."

"Who cares who kills whom while we are bothered about Viswa?"

Someone suddenly questioned Viswa's father, "Are you in the habit of beating him?"

"Sometimes you can't help it."

Viswa's mother said, "Whenever his teacher came and reported something, you lost your head ..." and burst into tears. "Teachers are an awful lot, you must pay no attention to what they say."

"But unless the teacher is strict young fellows can never be tamed."

Viswa's mother said sobbing, "You thrashed him

when that awful man came and said something."

"He had thrown cowdung on the master when he was not looking."

"You slapped," said the mother.

"I only patted his cheek." Everyone nursed a secret fear that Viswa had drowned in the river. Then the whole company trooped out, stood before the God in the temple hall, prayed and promised offerings if Viswa came back alive. If Bala had announced what she knew, it would have been a relief to everyone but she remained dumb.

* * *

As time passed Bala found existence a sore trial. She was no longer the little girl in a pig-tail, dressed in a cotton skirt and jacket. Now she had reached maturity – rather stocky with no pretensions to any special beauty except the natural charm of full-blown womanhood, she could not pass down the *agraharam* street without people staring at her and whispering comments behind her back. Sometimes some friend of the family would stop her on her way to the temple and ask, "Any news? Do you hope he will come back?" She found it a strain to be inventing answers. She snapped at her questioners sometimes but it made things worse. "Where is he?" people persisted in demanding. She said one day, "In Kashmir, making a lot of money, has sent a message to say he will be back soon."

"Who brought the message?" She invented a name. Next time when they questioned her again, she just said, "He has gone there as a priest in some temple." She soon tired of it all and showed herself outside home as little as possible, except for a visit to the temple on Tuesday and Friday evenings. She would gaze on the image in the sanctum when the camphor flame was waved to the ringing of the bells and prayed, "Oh, Lord. I don't even know whether my husband is alive. If he is alive, help me reach him. If he is dead, please let me die of cholera quickly." Other women looked at her strangely and asked among themselves, "Why is her mother not coming with her? There must be some reason. They are not on talking terms. She must be hiding something. He is no more but they are keeping it a secret. Instead of shaving her head and wearing white, she oils and combs her hair and decks it with flowers! And comes to the temple with *kumkum* on her brow, pretending to be a *sumangali*. A widow who pretends to be otherwise pollutes the temple precinct and its holiness is lost. She should be prohibited from entering the temple unless she shaves her head and observes the rules. Her mother must be a brazen woman to allow her out like this. We should talk to the priest."

The priest of the temple visited them one afternoon. Bala's mother was all excitement at the honour, unrolled a mat, seated him, offered him fruits and milk and made a lot of fuss. The priest accepted it all and looked around cautiously and asked in a hushed voice, "Where is your daughter?" Bala generally retired to a backroom when there was a visitor but listened to their talk. The priest was saying: "I remember Bala as a child, in fact I remember her wedding." He paused and asked, "Where is her husband, that boy who married her? I notice Bala at the temple some evenings." Her mother was upset and was not able to maintain the conversation. The priest said: "You know the old proverb: 'You may seal the mouth of a furnace, but not the mouth of gossip.' Till you get some proof to say he is living, it is better that you don't send Bala to the temple. Its sanctity must be preserved, which is my duty; otherwise as a priest of the temple, my family will face God's wrath." At this point of their talk Bala rushed out like a storm, her face flushed, "You people think I am a widow? I am not. He is alive

like you. I'll not rest until I come back with him some day and shame you all." She threw a word of cheer to her mother and flounced out of the house.

Bala's mother tried to follow her down the street but Bala was too fast for her. People stood and stared at the mother-daughter chase. Bala halted. When her mother came up she whispered, "Go back home. People are watching us. Keep well, I will come back. Remember that the priest is waiting in our house," Mother was in a dilemma. She halted as Bala raced forward, dashed in and out of the temple before anyone should notice her. She rushed past all the gaping men and women, past all rows of houses to Chariot Nook to Viswa's house and knocked. Her mother-in-law opened the door and was aghast, "Bala ! You look like *Kali* ... what is the matter ? Come in first. You should stay with us."

"Yes, when I come with my husband. She took a pinch of vermilion from a little bowl on a stand and pressed it on her brow, fell prostrate at her mother-in-law's feet, touched them reverentially, sprang back and was off even as the lady was saying, "Your father-in-law will come back soon, wait ..." Before her sentence was completed, Bala was gone.

Up to this point, my grandmother remembered

her mother's narration. Beyond this, her information was hazy. She just said, "Bala must have gone to the village cart-stand in the field beyond the last street, where travellers and bullock carts assembled. Bala must have paid for a seat in a carriage, travelled all night and reached a nearby town. Even in her hurry, before leaving home she did not forget to pack a small bag with a change of clothes, some money she had saved out of her birthday and other gifts, a few gold ornaments, and above all a knife in case she had to protect her honour and end her life. At the town she stayed in a choultry where an assortment of travellers and pilgrims was lodged. Her mind harped on a single word: Pandaripur. She made constant enquiries of everyone she came across and set forth in that direction. After many false starts, she got on the right track and joined travellers going on foot or by some mode of transport and reached Poona about a year later."

* * *

My grandmother's account had many gaps from this point onward. How Bala survived, what happened to her mother and where was her father all the while? What happened to Viswa's parents? Above all, why did she go to Poona to search for her husband? What led her steps to Poona? These questions never got an answer. My grandmother only snapped: "Why do you ask me? Am I a wizard to see the past? If you interrupt me like this, I'll never be able to complete the story. I can only tell you what I have heard from my mother. I just listened, without interrupting her as you do now. If you don't shut your mouth and keep only your ears open, I'll never tell you anything more. You can't expect me to know everything. If you want all sorts of useless information about the past, I cannot help you. Not my business. Whenever my mother felt like it, she would gather us around and tell her story – so that we might realize how strong and bold she was at one time. She would boast, 'You only see me as a cook at home, feeding you and pampering your father's whims and moods but at one time I could do other things which you, petted and spoilt children, could never even imagine.'"

* * *

By the time Bala reached Poona, she had exhausted all her gold and cash and was left with nothing. She felt terrified and lonely. People looked strangely different and spoke a language she did not understand. She reached a public rest house, a charity institution where *roti* was distributed, and held out her hand along with the others and swallowed whatever she got in order to survive. She made the rest house the central point and wandered about studying the faces of passers-by, hoping to spot out Viswa. She feared that if he had grown a beard, she would not be able to recognize him. All that she could remember was the head peeping over the wall and the black patch under his left ear, which he boasted would make him king – perhaps he was now the king of this town. She thought in her desperation of stopping some kindly soul to ask: "Who is the king here?" But they might take her to be a madcap and stone her.

The bazaars were attractive and she passed her time looking at the display of goods. She was afraid to move about after dusk for fear of being mistaken for a loose woman soliciting custom. She returned to the rest house and stayed there.

One day she was noticed by an elderly lady who asked in Marathi, "Who are you? I see you here every day. Where are you from? What is the matter?" Of course Bala could not understand her language, but felt it was all sympathy from a stranger and was moved to tears. The old woman took her hand and led her out of the rest house to her home nearby where men, women and children, surrounded her, joked and laughed. To their questions, all that she could answer was to point to the *thali* around her neck. They understood she was a married woman. When they questioned her further, she burst involuntarily into tears and uncontrollably into Tamil. She made up in gesticulation whatever she felt to be lacking in her Tamil explanation. She said, "My fate ..." She etched with her forefinger on her brow: "It's written here that I must struggle and suffer. How I have survived these months which I have lost count of, God alone knows. Here I have come to this strange city and I have to behave like a deaf-mute, neither understanding what you say nor making myself understood." They listened to her lamentation sympathetically without understanding a word, only realizing that it was a deeply felt utterance. Someone in the crowd recognizing the sound of the language asked, "*Madarasi*?"

"Must be so, she doesn't cover her head" said another. Bala could guess the nature of the query and nodded affirmatively. "I can take you to a man who came here many years ago. He may understand you." He beckoned her to follow him. She indicated that she wanted a drink of water, feeling her throat parched after her harangue.

A boy was deputed to guide her. She followed him blindly, not knowing or caring where she was going. The boy took her through the main street past the bazaars and crowds but proved too fast, running ahead. It was difficult to keep pace with him. She was panting with the effort. "Where are you taking me?" she asked again and again, but he only grinned and indicated some destination. Finally she found herself under an archway with a path leading to a big house. Leaving her there, the boy turned round and ran off before she could question him, perhaps feeling too shy to be seen with a woman. She was puzzled since there was no one in sight.

Beyond the archway and gate there was a garden. Presently a gardener appeared above a cluster of plants. He looked at her for a moment and stooped down again to resume his digging. Not knowing what to do next, she sat down on a sentry platform beside the arch, felt drowsy and shut her eyes. She woke up when she heard the sound of a horse trotting. She saw the rider pass under the arch and dismount in front of the house, helped by an attendant. He had thrown a brief glance at her in passing. He was dressed in breeches and embroidered vest and crowned with a turban – very much a man of these parts. Rather lean and of medium height. Could this be the man from the Tamil Land? Seemed unlikely. She did

not know what should be her next step. She continued to sit there. A little later, she noticed him again coming out on his horse. She was all attention now, staring at him when he passed under the arch. She noticed his moustache curving up to his ears. He threw at her another brief glance and passed. She decided to sit through and wait indefinitely, hoping to find some identification mark next time. She invoked the God in their village temple and prayed: "Guide me, Oh Lord! I don't know what to do ..." A couple of hours later the horse and the rider appeared and once again he threw at her the briefest glance and passed.

An attendant in livery approached her from the house. He asked, "Who are you? Master has seen you sitting here. Go away, don't sit here. Otherwise he will be angry and call the *kotwal*. Go away." She shook her head and sat immobile.

"Go away ..." He gestured her to go. He kept saying, "*Kotwal, kotwal,* he will come and take you to prison." She would not move. The servant looked intimidated by her manner and backed away. Ten minutes later he reappeared and asked her to follow him. She felt nervous wondering what sort of a male she was going to encounter. The front steps seemed endless and she felt weak at the knees and crossed the threshold expecting the worst. The man lounging in a couch watched her enter. She could not understand whether this was the beginning or the end of her troubles. She tried to study his face. There was not even a remote resemblance between the head she last saw over the wall and this man. He had no turban on and he was bald on top though his whiskers reached up to his earlobes. Gazing at his face she wondered what would happen if she made a dash for his whisker and lifted it to look for the black patch below his left ear; this might prove conclusive and the end of her quest. While she toyed with the idea, he thundered in Marathi, "Who are you? Why do you sit at my gate?"

She said, "They said that you speak Tamil." He shook his head. Took out his purse and held out some money and tried to wave her off. She refused the money. He summoned a servant to show her out. She sat down on the floor and refused to move. "They said you are from the South. Keep me here. I have nowhere to go. I am an orphan. I will be your servant, cook for you and serve you. Only grant me a shelter." He gave an order to the servant, suddenly got up, went upstairs and shut himself in a room. She began to doubt her wisdom in depending upon the urchin who guided her. So far this man had shown no sign of understanding Tamil in which she was addressing him. He had no identifiable feature except the greenish colour of his eyes, something that did not alter with years. She felt it might be wiser to sneak away quietly.

The servant fetched two *kotwals* who stood over and commanded her to get up. She felt she was making a hideous mistake in accosting a stranger and they were likely to think she was a characterless black-mailer. As the *kotwals* were trying to move her physically, she screamed in Tamil, "Don't touch me, I will reduce you to ashes. (*Thoddade, unnai posikiduven.*)" She looked fierce and the *kotwals*, though fiercer in a grotesque uniform and headgear, shrank back. While this was going on entered a woman nearing middle age and authoritative. She scowled at the men and cried, "What are you doing? Leave her alone." They tried to explain but she dismissed them instantly. She helped Bala to rise to her feet, seated her in a chair and asked: "Who are you? I heard you speak. Do you not understand our language?" Bala shook her head.

The other woman asked in Tamil: "Who are you?

At this point, Bala had the shrewdness to conceal her purpose and just said: "I came with some pilgrims to fulfill a vow at Pandaripur, got stranded and separated from a group." And spun a story which fell on sympathetic ears. "You are fortunate to live in a home like this, so comfortable and beautiful with its garden," said Bala.

"Yes, we love plants." She pointed upstairs, "He is a keen gardener himself. When my father lived, he had no time left. All his hours he spent in his shop and came home late at night. After my husband joined us, my father got some relief." Bala refrained from asking any question for fear of betraying her purpose but allowed the other to ramble on, gathering much information. She was on the point of asking his name but checked herself as the woman referred to him only as "He" or "Bhatji". Suddenly Surma cried, "Oh, how thoughtless of me to be sitting and talking like this without even asking if you are hungry! Come in with me." She got up and led Bala to the kitchen, lifted the lid off some vessels, bustled about, picked up a plate, set it on a little platform and put up a sitting plank and said, "Sit down and eat. I have something still left. We are both poor eaters. He is so busy at the shop, he seldom eats at home – only at night. I make something for myself. Don't like to spend too much time cooking. I also sit in the shop part of the day, especially when he has to go on his rounds. He is an expert in judging diamonds and all gems. His advice and appraisal is sought by everyone in this city. We have a large collection of precious stones ... apart from getting our supply from the mines in this country, we also import .. he has to go to Bombay sometimes when ships arrive at the port."

She fed Bala, which revived her since she had had nothing to eat after a couple of free *rotis* and a tumbler of water in the morning. She became loquacious and spirited. She washed the dishes at the backyard well and restored them to the kitchen shelf. The lady took her round the house and the garden. "My father built this in those days when we could engage many servants who kept the house clean, but now we have only ten. He always rests upstairs. Shall we go up and see the rooms there?"

Bala said, "Later, let us not disturb him now."

"Come, I'll show you your room. You should stay with us. Have you left your box in the rest house? Let us go and fetch it."

Bala said, "I came only with a small bag, but that was stolen on the way. Robbers set upon us and took away everything."

"My first glimpse of Bhatji was when he came into our shop one morning long ago," said Surma: "My father, with his eye glass stuck on one eye, was selecting diamonds for a party. I was minding something else, bent over a desk. He was standing at the entrance – how long I could not say. When I looked up he was there. There were people passing in and out of the shop, he was unnoticed. When the shop was clear of the crowd, he was still there at the doorway. I asked, 'What do you want? Who are you?' There was something about his person that touched my heart. He was lanky and looked famished. My first impulse was to rush to his help in some way, but I held myself back. I was a young woman of over eighteen years, he might be older. Somehow I felt attracted to this lean boy with hair falling on his nape untended, covering his forehead and unshaven face. It must have been months and years since a barber came near him. 'Father!' I called suddenly, 'Here is a boy waiting since the morning.' It was a propitious moment since father, instead of losing his temper, as was his habit whenever anyone stepped into the shop without any business (he was suspicious of youngsters particularly), took off the eye-glass, and asked mildly, 'What do you want?' He answered promptly, 'I want to work' in Marathi and then gave an account of himself. How he had started from a southern village, travelled up and about, visiting other parts of the country, working his way ...

"'How did you learn our language?'

" 'I was in Bombay and learnt it.' Father took to him kindly. He asked him to step in and questioned him in detail. Father enjoyed the narration

of the boy's adventures in other cities and his descriptions fascinated him. That a village boy from far off south should have had the courage to go out as far as Delhi (which was beyond father's dreams) and survive seemed to my father a great achievement. He engaged him immediately as a handyman, gave him a room above our shop and arranged for his food and other comforts.

"Very soon he became my father's right hand man, doing a variety of jobs in and out of the office and shop. He relieved father of a lot of strain and understood not only the nature of the trade but a lot about gems, their qualities and value. Father was impressed with the boy's intelligence and the ease with which he could be trained. Within six months he left a lot of responsibilities to him, trusting him absolutely. At the earliest opportunity my father set a barber on him and made him presentable with his head shaved in the front, leaving an elegant little tuft on top. Later, after we married, I induced him to grow whiskers so that he might have a weighty appearance. My father did not approve of our proposal to marry at first. He threatened to throw him out not only from our shop but from this country itself and ordered me not to talk to him and confined me at home. I had a miserable time. We eloped to Nasik and were married in the temple of Triambaka – a sort of marriage, quiet and private.

Eventually, father reconciled himself to the situation. When he died the gem business and the house fell to my share."

Surma constantly expressed her admiration and love for Viswanath: "When I saw him first, he was so young and timid; now he manages our business and is often called to the court and high places for consultations and supply of gems ..."

The story writer asked at this point: "Were they the only ones in that house?"

"Yes, must be so," said my grandmother.

"What happened to the rest of the family – there must surely have been other members of the family!"

"Why do you ask me? How do I know?" said my grandmother. "I can only tell the story as I heard it. I was not there as you know. This is about my father and mother who were still apart though living under the same roof."

I asked the next question, which bothered me as a story writer: "Did Surma Bai have no children?"

"I don't care if she had or had not or where they were, how is it our concern?"

"But you say they were living together for fifteen years!"

"What a question! How can I answer it? You must ask them. Anyway it is none of our business.

My mother mentioned Surma and only Surma and not a word about anyone else. If you want me to go on with the story, you must not interrupt me. I forget where I was ... I am only telling you what I know." She stopped her narration at this point and left in a huff to supervise her daughters-in-law in the kitchen.

Bala's opportune moment came when Surma said one evening, "I am joining some friends who perform *bhajans* (group singing) at the Krishna temple on Fridays. I will come back after it is over. You won't mind being alone?"

"Not at all," said Bala, "I'll look after the house and take care of everything."

"He is in his room, may come down if he wants anything ..."

"I'll take care of him, do not worry about him," said Bala reassuringly and saw her off in her *tonga* at the gate. The moment the *tonga* was out of sight she ran back into the house, shutting the front door, ran upstairs and entered Viswa's room. He was reclining on a comfortable couch reading a book. She shut the door behind her softly. He did not look up. He pretended to be absorbed in the book. She stood silently before him for a few moments, and then said, "What is the book that grips you so completely that you do not notice anyone entering your room?"

"What are you blabbering? Get out! You have no business to come up here."

"Oh, stop that tone. Don't pretend. Not good for you."

"Are you threatening me? I'll call the guard and throw you out."

"By all means. I know the guards. I am not what I was on the first day. I can speak to them myself. In fact, I am closer to them than you are. Call them and see what happens."

"Oh!" Viswa groaned. "Go away, don't bother me ..."

She said, "We must end this drama and how we are going to do it, I can't say now. But leave it at that." He pretended not to understand her language. But she said, "Your whiskers do not hide your face. If you lift the left one slightly, as you did the other day while washing your face, the black is still there, which had proved correct my guess and also what you said years ago when you peeped over the wall, that it was lucky and would make you a king. You are lucky, rich and favoured at the court ... I have waited long enough." She fingered her *thali* and said, "This can't lie. You knotted it in the presence of God." He protested again, "No, no, I don't know what you are saying," but she was hammering her point relentlessly.

Ultimately he was overwhelmed. "Be patient for some more time. Be as you are, Surma is a rare creature. We must not upset her."

"I will wait, but not forever." By the time Surma came back from the *bhajan*, she found nothing unusual. Bala was at her post in the kitchen. Viswa was in the garden trimming a jasmine plant. Once again Viswa and Bala took care to move in separate orbits in the house. Bala was in no hurry. Now that she had established her stand, she just left him alone until the next *bhajan* day when Surma was away. She said: "This can't go on much longer. We must go back."

"Go back where?" he asked in consternation.

"To our village, of course," she said calmly.

"Impossible!" he cried. "After all these years! I can't. I can't give up my trade."

"You may take your share and continue the business anywhere," she said calmly. She knew his weak point now and could exploit it fully. Any excitement or anger would spoil her plan. She was very clear in her mind about how she should carry out her scheme. She had worked out the details of the campaign with care, timing it in minute detail.

He knew it was going to be useless to oppose her. He pleaded, "I'll tell her the truth and you may continue here as my wife, and not as a domestic."

"I want to get back to our own place and live there. I have set a time limit; beyond that I won't stay, I'll go back."

"Certainly, I will make any arrangement you may want and send an escort to take you back home safely."

"You will be the escort, I'll not go with anyone else."

"Then stay here," he said. At this stage they had to stop their discussion, since they heard Surma return home. He felt nervous to remain alone with Bala and was terrified of her tactics.

"I can't live without Surma," he kept wailing.

"You will have to learn to live with your wife."

"Surma is also my wife."

"I know she is not. I know in this country it is not so easy. You have kept her, or rather she has kept you."

He realized in due course that there was no escape. He said, "Give me time. I'll see how we can manage it."

"I've given you all the time ... years and years. The trouble and the risk I have undergone to search you out, God alone is our witness! I am not going to allow it to go waste. I am taking you back even if you kill me. I have set the date of our departure – not later than the next Full Moon."

At their next meeting he said, "I can't survive without Surma, she must also come with us. I don't know how to tell her."

"Try to persuade her to stay back. We will have to tell her the facts. After all, you are going back to our legitimate home to your real wife."

"No, I can't. You don't know her nature. She will commit suicide."

"I will commit suicide if you do not come away. Which of us shall it be?"

He felt desperate and said, "I can't live without her. Let her also come with us. We shall go away. Show some consideration for my feelings also."

"Very well, if she doesn't agree to go with us?"

"Please don't drive me mad. Who asked you to come all the way to torment me like this?" At this point she lost her patience and left him.

When Surma asked him later: "You look rather tired and pale, shall I call the physician?" he demurred. But she lost no time in calling a physician who said, "He is disturbed. He must take medicine and rest. Something is troubling his mind."

Surma too became agitated: "I have never seen him so sick at any time. What could it be? He was all right." She put him to bed and stayed by his side, leaving all household work to Bala. Viswa tossed and groaned in bed. Bala carried food to his bedside upstairs. She made it unnecessary for Surma to come down except for her bath, food and *puja;* Surma then went up and sat by his side silently. The physician had given him some potion which acted as a sedative and put him to sleep.

Bala assumed an air of extreme gloom to match Surma's mood in sympathy. A week later she said, "Bhatji looks better. You should not fall sick moping at home. We will leave a guard at his side and go out for a little fresh air. Let us visit the temple and offer *puja* to Vitobha and stroll along the lake. You will feel refreshed."

"No. I can't leave him alone."

Four days later Bala repeated her suggestion and added, "Ask him, he may like you to go out for your own good. I am sure he will have as much concern for your welfare."

Surma eventually agreed. Bala said, "You must think of the shop too."

"Guru looks after the shop, he is a good man," Surma said. "He brings the accounts and reports every day, very dependable ..."

"Even then," Bala said, "You must go there or Bhatji can go as soon as possible. It'll also refresh him."

"True, he is worrying about the shop silently. I

do not know what to do ... I have never been in this predicament before."

When Guru came the next evening they went out in the *tonga,* leaving him in charge of Viswa. They visited the temple first and then went on to the lake. Strolling round the lake, which reflected the setting sun, Bala cried, "Oh, see how beautiful! See those birds diving in."

"I wish I could enjoy the scene and the breeze but my mind is troubled. How I wish Bhatji were well ... his normal self, riding his horse, sitting in the shop with his diamonds and customers; then I could sit here and watch the lake with a free mind."

"He must travel and go out for a change ... We could plan for a three or four month's absence. Guru and his son could look after the shop. That will make a new man of Bhatji."

"Where can we go?"

"We may go south, so many temples we could visit – I have especially in mind Gunasekaram where mental sickness is cured miraculously through offerings and *puja* to that God."

"We can't, so far away and so long it'll take!"

Bala did not continue, but left the subject at that. But she repeated the suggestion whenever she found a chance. Surma thought it over and discussed the matter with Viswa and worked out the details and settled on a date for the journey after consulting their astrologer and physician.

"I remember," said Ammani, "my mother mention that they were carried in two *palanquins* and had a retinue of bearers who took over in relays at different stages, and many torch-bearers and lance men to protect them from robbers and wild animals when they crossed jungles in the mountain ghats. Arrangements for the journey were made by Surma and Viswa, who had influence at the court and got the *Peshwa's* support. I am sure the *Peshwa* sent word to his vassals and subordinates along the route to protect and help the party. On the day fixed, Bala and party began their journey, arrived about a month later in Bangalore and camped in the rest house on a tank bund. I think from the description it is the same tank known as the Sampangi* today."

They camped for three days. All the three were very happy; Bala because she was on the way home, Viswa because they had succeeded in persuading Surma to undertake the tour, and Surma because Viswa already looked better and eagerly anticipated the visit to the temples. He did not wish to think of the future beyond.

---

* *Actually at present, it is Nehru Stadium, the tank having been drained many years ago.*

On the fourth day they wound up the camp, all packed and ready to start onward. Bala however had made up her mind differently. From the rest house one set of steps led up to the highway where the *palanquins* were waiting. All other members of the party, the bearers and guards, Surma and Viswa went up the steps. Bala however lagged behind, suddenly turned right about and went down the steps leading to the water's edge. At first they did not notice her. When they reached the road Surma asked, while climbing into their *palanquin,* "Where is Bala?"

Viswa said: "She seems to be taking her own time. Probably a last minute wash. Let us start. We should reach the next stage before nightfall. She will follow." The bearers had lifted the *palanquin* containing Surma and Viswa.

Viswa still hesitated and said, "Stop! I see that she is going down the steps. Why?"

Surma said, "It looks to me strange. Oh, God, she has stepped into the water. Oh, stop!" she said in alarm when she heard Bala's scream: "I'm drowning ... Viswa come for a moment." Viswa jumped off the *palanquin* and reached the water's edge. By that time Bala stood neck-deep in water. Viswa shrieked in alarm: "What are you doing?"

She replied with the water lapping her chin, "I am not coming with you."

"Are you mad? Why this scene?" He made a move to go down and pull her up.

She said, "If you take another step, I'll go down. Stay where you are and listen. No, don't come near, you can hear me where you are."

"All right, I won't come forward. Don't stand in the water, come up and speak."

"I won't come up until you turn Surma back to Poona."

Surma had meanwhile come down and was standing behind Viswa: "What! What have I done to you that you should say this?"

"You have been like a goddess to me, but I can't go home with you. Our village will not accept you. I am Viswa's wife. You see this *thali* was knotted by him. He is my husband, I can't share him with you."

Surma was shocked, "We were such good friends! Let me also drown with you."

At this Viswa held her back firmly. Bala said, "Viswa, take her with you and leave me alone. I am already shivering and will die of cold – if you don't make up your mind quickly whether you want me or Surma. Send her back honourably home. Let the *palanquins* be turned around with her, if you want to save me."

They pleaded, appealed and shed tears but the *palanquins* and the entourage had to run around and head for Poona before Bala would come out. She did not want any of Surma's entourage to stay back.

"Ammani," I (this writer) said, "I can't find any excuse for the way your mother manoeuvred to get rid of the other woman. Your mother was too deep and devious for the poor lady, who had shown so much trust in her, whom she had sheltered and nourished when she was in desperate straits, not to mention the years she cared for and protected Viswa who had after all strayed his way to Poona and was literally a tramp at the start ..."

"Don't talk ill of your ancestors. Not right. He was not a tramp but a respected merchant and official at the *Peshwa's* court," Ammani retorted.

"He had only been a lowly clerk in her father's shop, remember?"

"What of it? Whatever it is, he rose high because of his mettle."

"And mainly through Surma's support – he should have remembered it at the time he yielded to your mother's coercive tactics."

"What else could a poor woman like her do to recover her husband? Only a woman can understand it. To a woman, her husband is everything. She can't lose him. Remember in what condition

Bala had left home and what trials she must have gone through to reach Poona and how much misery she faced before she could reach him! Everything is justified, all means are justified in her case. Did not Savitri conquer Yama himself, and trap him into promising her a boon? And the boon she asked for was to beget children and he had to give her his blessing that she should have children. After accepting the boon, she asked how it would be possible when he as the God of Death was carrying away her husband's life, leaving his inert body in the forest – and then Yama had to yield back Satyavan's life. You could not imagine a greater woman than Savitri for austerity and purity of mind."

"Still I am unable to accept your mother's tactics – she could have adopted some other method."

"Such as?" she said suppressing her irritation.

"She could have revealed that she was his wife on the first day itself."

"Surma would have bundled her off or got rid of her in some manner."

"Would not Viswa have protected her?"

"No, he was completely under her spell at that time."

"Was it necessary to drag the poor woman with false promises up to Bangalore? Could they not have managed it in some other way?"

"Such as?" she asked again.

"I don't know. I'd have thought of more honourable ways."

"You cannot manipulate people in real life as you do in a story," she said.

As my remarks incensed her, she refused to continue her story and abruptly got up with the excuse, "I have better things to do at this time than talk to a fellow like you ..." For nearly a week she ignored me while I followed her about with my notebook. She ignored me until I pleaded, "You must please complete the story. I want to hear it fully. You know why?"

"Why?"

"Otherwise I will be born a donkey in my next *janma*."

"How do you know?"

"The other day I attended a Ramayana discourse. A man got up in the middle of the narrative and tried to go out of the assembly but the *pundit* interrupted himself to announce, "It's said in the *Shastras* that anyone who walks out in the middle of a discourse will be a donkey in his next birth', and the man who was preparing to leave dropped plump back in his seat when he heard it. And so please ..."

"Tomorrow evening. I'm going to be busy today." Next evening after she had pottered around her garden and had her evening cold bath and said her prayers, she summoned me to the hall, took her seat on the swing and continued her story.

* * *

At Bangalore the parting of ways was harrowing. Surma, always so assured, positive and a leader, broke down and humbled herself to the extent of saying, "Let me only go with you. I have surrendered Viswa to you, only let me be near you. I have loved you as a friend. I'll come with you and promise to return to Poona after visiting the temples. Please show me this consideration. I accept with all my heart that he is your husband. I'll never talk to him again or look at him even. But let me be with you ... Viswa, talk to her please."

Viswa turned to Bala and said, "Let her come with us. She will visit the temples and go back. I promise."

Bala stood thinking for a while, wept a little, controlled herself and said firmly to Surma, "No, it won't be possible. In our place we will be hounded out. I'll advise Viswa to go with you, anywhere, back to Poona or forward. Only leave me alone. You have got to choose."

It was pathetic and humiliating with their retinue and *palanquin-bearers* watching the scene. Bala put her arms around Surma, rested her head on her shoulder and then sobbing, bowed down and prostrated at her feet, got up and moved away from her towards the tank again, whereupon Surma cried desperately, "Don't! don't! I am leaving. May God bless you both." She hurried up her retinue and got into her *palanquin* and left while Bala stood on the last step of the tank and watched. Viswa stood dumbstruck, not knowing what to do. That was the last they saw of Surma. She was not heard of again: whether she went back home to Poona or ended her misery by walking into the next available tank on the way, no one in my family knew.

Viswa would have frantically raced behind the *palanquins* but for the check of Bala's stare in silence. They stayed in the same rest house for three more days, waiting to join other travellers going south. Meanwhile Bala summoned a barber and persuaded Viswa to shave off his whiskers, saying, "In our part of the country you will be taken for a ghoul and children will run away screaming at the sight of you." She stood away from him after the shave and observed,

"Now I can recognize you better. The patch under the ear is intact. I am doubly assured now – the same features which I used to see over the backyard wall, only filled up with age. Whatever made you hide such a fine face behind a wilderness of hair!"

"At the *Peshwa's* court it was customary and considered necessary."

★ ★ ★

At this point Ammani interrupted herself to warn me: "Don't ask how long they took to reach their village. All I can say is ultimately they did reach it." Only the river was there and the temple stood solidly as ever, but the old priest whose remarks had driven Bala out of her home and to whom she vowed to prove that her husband was alive was not there. The temple had a new priest who did not remember the old families. All the same, the very first thing Bala did was to enter the temple and stand before the God with her husband, praying for continued grace. She ordered an elaborate ritual of prayers and offerings and distributed food and fruits and cash to a little gathering of men, women and children. Viswa had left the place thirty years, and Bala about twenty years, before. Most of the

landmarks were gone, also the people. Bala went back to her old house in the 4th street and found some strangers living in it, who said, "We bought this house from an old woman who went to live her last days in Kasi after her husband's death. Their only daughter had run away from home and was not heard of again."

Viswa searched for his old house but could not locate it. That neighbourhood had been demolished and he could not find anyone to answer his questions, except a man grazing his cow, who just said, "Ask someone else. I know nothing." Viswa tried here and there, but could get no news of his parents or his relatives. The village seemed to have been deserted by all the old families. Bala's main purpose to visit the temple and offer *puja* to Ranganatha accomplished, she saw no reason for staying in the village. They decided to move to a nearby town where Viswa could establish himself as a gem merchant and start a new life.

* * *

At this point I could not get my grandmother to specify which town it was. If I pried further, she said, "I was not born then, remember that fact."

"What was that town? Could it be Trichy?"

"Maybe," she said.

"Or Kumbakonam?"

"Maybe," she said again.

"Or Tanjore?"

"Why not?" she said mischievously.

"Or Nagapattinam?"

"I was not born. How could I know? I tell you again and again – but you question me as if I could see the past."

"From your village, the nearby town must have been within fifty or a hundred miles. Have you not heard your mother mention any special landmark like a river or a temple?"

"She only mentioned that the river Kaveri was flowing and it was a place with several temples; she mentioned that every evening she could visit a temple, a different one each day of the week."

"Let us take it as Kumbakonam. Where did your marriage take place?"

"On a hill temple, not far from where we lived."

"It must be Swami Malai in Kumbakonam. Were you so ignorant as not to notice where you were being married?"

"I was eleven and followed my parents."

"Extraordinary!" I said, which offended her and she threatened to stop her narration. But I pleaded with her to continue. I realized that she knew it was Kumbakonam but was only teasing me.

★ ★ ★

Viswanath established himself as a gem expert in Kumbakonam. He acquired a house not far from the river. He sat in a small room in the front portion of his house and kept his wares in a small bureau, four feet high, half glazed.

(The heirloom is still with the family. When I was young I was given that little bureau for keeping my school books and odds and ends. I had inscribed in chalk on the narrow top panel of this bureau, 'R.K. Narayanaswami B.A., B.L. Engine Driver'. My full name with all the honours I aspired for, I wonder if one can detect any trace of that announcement now. I have not seen the heirloom for many years.)

Viswa's reputation spread as an expert appraiser of gems. People brought him diamonds for evaluation and to check for flaws. Through an eye glass he examined the stone and gave his verdict before they were handed over to the goldsmith for setting.

Bala turned out to be a model wife in the orthodox sense, all trace of her adventurous spirit or independence completely suppressed. One could hardly connect her with the young woman who had tramped all alone across hundreds of miles in search of her husband and succeeded in bringing him back home – dominating, devious and aggressive, till she attained her object. Now she was docile and never spoke to her husband in the presence of others. Her tone was gentle and subdued. It was a transformation.

She wore an eighteen-cubit length of silk sari in the orthodox style, instead of the twelve-cubit cotton wrap favoured in Poona. She wore diamond earrings, decked herself in a heavy gold necklace and bangles and applied turmeric on her cheeks and a large vermilion mark on her forehead. She rose at five in the morning, walked to the river, bathed and washed her saris, took them home for drying, filled a pitcher and carried it home, also drew several pails of water from the well in their backyard to fill a cauldron for domestic purposes.

She circumambulated the sacred *tulasi* plant in the backyard and then sat down in the *puja* room with lamps lit and chanted *mantras* and by the time Viswa woke up at six, lit the kitchen fire and prepared his morning porridge or anything else he needed for breakfast. She cooked for him twice a day, buying vegetables from a woman who brought them to their door in a basket. She went to the temples in the evening with offerings and oil for the lamps in the shrines.

* * *

Their first born came two years later – a daughter, and another daughter, and then another daughter – "that is myself," said my grandmother. The fourth was a son.

The next twenty years, roughly, were years of prosperity. Viswa's business flourished. In proper time, he found bridegrooms for his daughters and sent his son Swaminathan to study in Madras at the Medical College; he was among the first batch of Indians qualified for the medical profession.

Viswa was past sixty when he found himself isolated. His daughters were married and gone. "I was the youngest and last to leave home," said Ammani. "My husband (your grandfather) was a sub-magistrate and posted to work in different villages of our district – here, there and everywhere, until we came to rest in Madras after his retirement. We bought this house in which we find ourselves now, he also acquired a number of other houses in this street, and bungalows in the western area on Kelly's Road, agricultural lands somewhere, and a garden. (The garden was known as *Walker Thottam* and supplied vegetables to the wholesale market at Kotawal Chavadi in George Town.) And all his time was taken up in managing his estates."

"You said he was started on less than fifty rupees. How did you manage to buy so many houses and lands?" I asked.

"We did not actually have to depend upon his pay."

"Oh, I understand. I will not question you further."

"Even if you asked, I wouldn't be able to explain how a magistrate earned – money just poured in, I think. We had a brougham and horse, a coachman and so much of everything. My own family consisted of three daughters and two sons. The eldest daughter was married and died in Madurai and my family was reduced to four. Your mother was my second daughter ... I always felt that the kind of wealth your grandfather amassed was illusory, because within six months of your grandfather's death, by a court decree all his property was lost through a foolish business venture of his in steel. His trusted partner declared insolvency and fled to Pondicherry and your grandfather's properties were attached and auctioned to make good a bank loan – something to do with the notorious Arbuthnot Bank crash."

"Even this house was nearly gone but for the help of a neighbour, who loaned us five thousand rupees to redeem it at the last moment. Our creditors had already stuck notices of auction on our door, and by beat of tom-tom and loud announcements were inviting bidders. Crowds gathered at our door. You were due to be delivered in a couple of weeks, but the bustle, crowd and tom-tom beats were nerve-racking and affected your mother, who had come for her confinement and was in a delicate state of pregnancy. She became panic-stricken and got labour pains in that excitement. Your birth was rather premature. Only this house was saved of all your grandfather's properties – thanks, as I mentioned, to the last minute help of our neighbour Mr. Pillai who lived in Number Two Vellala Street."

(One morning, two years ago, I had a desire to revisit Number One Vellala Street in Purasawalkam, where all of us were born in one particular room. We habitually considered the house as the focal point of the entire family scattered in other districts, visiting it from time to time. My friend Ram of *The Hindu* was also curious to see the house and the environs mentioned in MY DAYS. One morning we drove down to Vellala Street in Purasawalkam, but found no trace of the old house. It was totally demolished, cleared and converted into a vacant plot on which the idea was to build an air-conditioned multi-storeyed hotel.

Among the debris we found the old massive main-door lying with "One" still etched on it. Ram made an offer on the spot and immediately transported it to his house, where it is mounted as a show-piece.)

* * *

To go back to the main theme. Changes were coming in Viswa's life. His son Dr. Swaminathan was appointed District Medical Officer at Kolar in Mysore State.

When Dr. Swaminathan left for Kolar, Viswa and Bala missed their children and found life dull. Viswa, now nearing seventy, worked less, finding it tedious to continue his gem business. He felt irritated when customers came for advice and discouraged them. Gradually he stopped all business, although his little bureau had a stock of precious stones.

Bala too had become rather tired and engaged a cook, a woman, who brought along with her a twelve year old daughter. Bala found their company diverting. The woman, who had been a destitute, now felt she had found a home and worked hard, relieving Bala of a lot of drudgery. Gradually, Bala preferred to lounge in bed, hardly stirring out, leaving the management of the house to the woman and her daughter.

Viswa too stationed himself all day in an easy chair on the *veranda* over-looking the street. Bala often implored him to go out and meet his cronies in the neighbourhood who used to gather in the temple corridor, sit around and chat after a *darshan* of the God. But now he never went out, secretly worried about Bala's declining health. He sent for the *vaid*, who came every other day, studied her pulse and prescribed a medicine, a concoction of rare herbs, he claimed. Viswa wrote a letter to his son expressing anxiety, but official work kept Dr. Swaminathan busy. He could come only four weeks later. When he found his mother's condition serious, he struggled hard to retrieve her but with all the medicines and needles in his bag, he could not save her.

"When the obsequies were over, my brother and sisters returned to their respective places. My husband was a magistrate in Tindivanam. I had two daughters at that time and we also left."

Viswanath was persuaded to go to Kolar with his son. The house was practically locked up, with one or two rooms left open for the woman, with her daughter, to live there as a care-taker on a monthly salary.

Viswanath's life entered yet another phase: he had to live in Kolar with his son, whose family consisted of his wife, a daughter and a son, both under ten. At first Viswa had protested and resisted, but the doctor persuaded him to wind up his establishment in Kumbakonam.

At Kolar Dr. Swaminathan lived in a bungalow set in a spacious compound. Viswa enjoyed an early morning walk in the compound and then inspected the kitchen garden in the backyard, and from the *veranda* watched the birds and trees, watched his two grandchildren going off to a nearby mission school, and his son leaving for the hospital in the morning. He turned in at noon for his bath and then said his prayers in the *puja* room. His daughter-in-law, although reserved and formal, looked after his comforts and needs hour-to-hour. He had a room and he enjoyed his siesta after lunch. In spite of all the comfort and security, he missed Bala and felt a vacuity at times. "No one can take her place," he often told himself. Sometimes he thought of Surma too but the intensity of feeling was gone; it was just a faded memory revived with effort, without any pangs of recollection. His son, the doctor, was a busy man having to attend the Government Hospital as well as administer medical services in the whole district and he had to be away on 'circuits' frequently.

Viswa felt proud of his son, especially at the beginning when he brought his salary home and handed over the cash, about four hundred rupees, in a net bag. Viswa carried it in after counting the amount, and called his daughter-in-law, "Lakshmi, come and take charge of this cash. Count it properly and spend it wisely. You must also build up savings. I want nothing of this. I have no use for this cash. I have my own. This is all yours, keep it safely." This was a routine statement every month. He awaited the salary-day month after month and the routine continued.

He was happy as long as it continued, but when the practice was gradually given up for practical reasons and Swami began to hand his monthly salary directly to his wife, Viswa became resentful secretly. He tried to overcome it, hoping that next time or the next time, Swami would resume the courtesy of recognizing his presence when he brought home the salary. This was probably a temporary aberration or an absent-minded lapse. Viswa bore it for three months. At the end of it, he said to himself: "I'll intercept him tomorrow evening when he comes in with the salary. I will not leave the *veranda* until he arrives, test whether he'll hand me the bag or still give it to his wife." Brooding over it, he had magnified the situation and imparted an undue significance to it.

Next day Dr. Swaminathan did not come in the evening but at noon suddenly, and was in a great hurry. He did not enter the house but called from outside, "Lakshmi." When she emerged from the kitchen, he held out the salary bag from the *veranda.* "I can't come in now. People are waiting. We are off to a nearby village where ratfalls are reported." He rushed back to the medical team waiting at the gate in a horse carriage. They were to go out and investigate a possible outbreak of bubonic plague and inoculate the population.

Viswa, who had been gathering coriander leaves in the kitchen garden, came in with a sprig for seasoning the lunch items. Lakshmi presented to him the money bag. "What is this?"

"Salary. He brought it now."

Viswa glared at her, and asked, "Why at this hour? Why did he not call me?"

"He was in a hurry, people waiting at the gate."

"Oh!" he said, "He is a big man, is he?" and ignored the bag, dropped the coriander on the floor, marched off to his room and bolted the door, came out at lunch time, ate in grim silence, retired to his room again, sat on his bed and brooded: "He is becoming really indifferent. This morning he left without a word to me. All of them are behaving callously. Children get out and come in as they please. They don't notice me at all. Lakshmi thinks her duty is done after feeding

me as she would feed a dog without a word. The last three days Swami never spoke to me more than three sentences. They think I am an orphan depending on their favours. This is the curse of old age. I will teach them a lesson!"

He briskly made up a bundle of clothes, stuffed them in a small jute bag, put on his long grey shirt, seized his staff and started out. "Lakshmi," he called. She came out and was taken aback at the sight of him. He just said, "I am off ..." as he had said to Bala over the wall before absconding years before. That tendency seemed to be ingrained in his blood. "Where?" she asked timidly.

"Never mind where – did your husband tell me where he was going? That is all." He briskly got down the steps and was out, leaving the lady staring after him speechlessly. The children had gone out to school. He found his way to the railway station, waited for a train, got into it, changed trains and ultimately reached Kumbakonam and was back in his home in Salai Street – surprising the caretaker and her daughter.

My grandmother's actual words: "That was a disastrous step he took. What mad rage drove him to that extent no one could say. The caretaker and her daughter were not the kind he should have associated with. They were evil-minded, coming from a nearby village notorious for its evil practices such as fostering family intrigues, creating mischief and practising black magic. When my father knocked, they were rather surprised but welcomed him with a great show of joy. They fussed over him. They consulted him on what he liked to eat and cooked and fried things and bought choice vegetables and fruits to feed him. They washed his feet whenever he came in after a short visit outside. They treated him like a prince till he must have begun to think, 'My son and wife treated me like a tramp and hanger-on, not a day did anyone ask what I liked. They always restricted my eating with the excuse, "You should not eat this or that at your age." My son thought that as a doctor, he was *Brihaspathi* himself! They denied me all delicacies, whereas this woman and her daughter know what I want.' The house was filled all the time with the smell of frying – chips, *bondas, pakodas* and sweets. Viswa was a very contented man now. He had a sturdy constitution which withstood all the gluttony he was indulging in.

"One fine day we got information that he had married the caretaker's daughter in a quiet, simple ceremony conducted by the woman who managed to get a priest from her village. It was a culmination of his rage against his son. He could think of no better way to assert his independence. He was seventy-five and the girl was seventeen. He married her convinced that it would be the best way to shock and spite his family, all of whom seemed hostile to him."

Now the woman had him under her control, in course of time she took further steps to consolidate her position. She began to suggest that they were no longer mere caretakers of the house but his family, and that the young wife and her mother should be made the owners of the house through a deed of transfer. She found a pleader who prepared a document and presented it to Viswa for his signature. At this point he still had some sense left. He hesitated and delayed while his mother-in-law kept up her pressure – through persuasion, bullying and even starving him. He dodged the issue with some excuse or other, and began to wonder if he should not have continued in Kolar. He was losing his cheer and his young wife nagged him to sign the document.

They had their eyes on his stock of precious stones, which he always kept with him although he did no business now; he also had enough cash left but took care to keep it with a banking friend, drawing just the amount he needed at a time. This irked his mother-in-law who had aimed high; she now goaded her daughter to sulk and nag him at night. He dodged her by taking his bed-roll to the *pyol* on the excuse that he found the room too stuffy, thus evading his wife's pillow talk. He avoided her all through the day too while the mother-in-law murmured asides and remarks. He was beginning to brood and plan a return to Kolar. The thought of his son was exhilarating and Kolar seemed a paradise and a haven of peace.

The woman was shrewd and began to guess from his mood that he might slip away. She told her daughter, "I have to go to our village on some important work and will be back tomorrow. Keep a watch on your husband. Keep him in and shut the front door."

At their village the woman consulted the local wiseacre, explaining the difficulties her son-in-law was creating. The wiseacre's income was through his claims to magic, black or white, the exorcising of spirits and the making of potions and amulets. He said, "You must tell me frankly what you want. Don't hide anything." She explained that while she wanted her son-in-law to be friendly and amenable, he was becoming tough and hostile. She said tearfully, "Out of compassion for the fellow in dotage, I agreed to give him my daughter so tender and young. But he is becoming indifferent and ill-treats her. You must help me."

The wiseacre pretended to note down points and said, "Come next week and bring two sovereigns. I'll have to acquire some ingredients and herbs, which will cost you something. I won't charge you for my service, that's my guru's command." She went home thinking, "Only a week more."

When she came back to the village a week later, the wiseacre gave her a packet. "There are two pills in it. Give them both to him with his food. They are tasteless and will dissolve and when the pills get into his system, he'll follow his wife like a lamb and treat you as his guru."

The woman went back home gloating over the possibilities ahead, with the packet tucked in a sari at her waist. On the following Friday she prepared a special feast explaining that this Friday was particularly sacred for some reason. She was secretive about the pills and did not mention it even to her daughter, but planned to get him to sign the document next day after the pill was completely assimilated in his system, with the document ready at hand. Viswa, a confirmed glutton these days, was pleased and seemed relaxed, bantered with his wife and mother-in-law in anticipation of the feast saying, "This indeed is a pleasant surprise for me. What a lot of trouble you take!" The fragrance of delicacies emanating from the kitchen was overpowering. When the time came for lunch, the woman spread two long banana leaves side by side saying that the couple must dine together today, and heaped the leaves with item after item – the high point of the feast being almond and milk *payasam* in a silver bowl for him and in a brass cup for his wife. Before serving it, the woman managed to dissolve the two pills in the silver bowl.

My grandmother concluded, "That was the end. My husband was a sub-magistrate at Nagapattinam when we got information that Viswa's end had come suddenly. I have nothing more to add. Don't ask questions."

(My – this writer's – mother, Ammani's second daughter, who was ninety-three at the time of her death in 1974, used to maintain that she had a hazy recollection of being carried on the arms of her mother at Kumbakonam and witnessing a lot of hustle and bustle following a funeral, people passing in and out of the house and some boxes being locked and sealed by the police and a motley crowd milling around.)

I asked my grandmother, "What happened to that woman and your young step-mother?"

"I don't know. I have no idea."

"No inquest, no investigation, no questioning of that woman?"

"I don't know. We could not stay away from Nagapattinam too long since the Collector, an Englishman, was coming for inspection and the

magistrate was required to be present. We had to leave. My brother, Dr. Swaminathan, came down from Kolar and took charge of the situation and my father's assets. I can't tell you anything more about it. All I know is what I could gather from my brother later. He spoke to our neighbours who mentioned to him the woman's schemes; the pleader had a lot to say about that woman's ambition and manoeuvres to grab the wealth and property. My brother could not stay on for long either but before going back to Kolar he made some arrangement for the disposal of that house ... that's all we know."

* * *